P9-CRI-678

WELCOME TO
PASSPORT TO READING

A beginning reader's ticket to a brand-new world!

Every book in this program is designed to build read-along and read-alone skills, level by level, through engaging and enriching stories. As the reader turns each page, he or she will become more confident with new vocabulary, sight words, and comprehension.

These PASSPORT TO READING levels will help you choose the perfect book for every reader.

READING TOGETHER
Read short words in simple sentence structures together to begin a reader's journey.

READING OUT LOUD
Encourage developing readers to sound out words in more complex stories with simple vocabulary.

READING INDEPENDENTLY
Newly independent readers gain confidence reading more complex sentences with higher word counts.

READY TO READ MORE
Readers prepare for chapter books with fewer illustrations and longer paragraphs.

This book features sight words from the educator-supported Dolch Sight Words List. This encourages the reader to recognize commonly used vocabulary words, increasing reading speed and fluency.

For more information, please visit passporttoreadingbooks.com.

Enjoy the journey!

2017 © Universal Studios. Despicable Me 3 is a trademark and copyright of Universal Studios. Licensed by Universal Studios. All Rights Reserved.

Hachette Book Group supports the right to free expression and the value of copyright. The purpose of copyright is to encourage writers and artists to produce the creative works that enrich our culture.

The scanning, uploading, and distribution of this book without permission is a theft of the author's intellectual property. If you would like permission to use material from the book (other than for review purposes), please contact permissions@hbgusa.com. Thank you for your support of the author's rights.

Little, Brown and Company
Hachette Book Group
1290 Avenue of the Americas, New York, NY 10104
Visit us at lb-kids.com
www.despicable.me

First Edition: May 2017

Little, Brown and Company is a division of Hachette Book Group, Inc. The Little, Brown name and logo are trademarks of Hachette Book Group, Inc. The publisher is not responsible for websites (or their content) that are not owned by the publisher.

Library of Congress Control Number 2017935902

ISBNs: 978-0-316-50761-5 (pbk.), 978-0-316-50760-8 (ebook), 978-0-316-50758-5 (ebook), 978-0-316-50759-2 (ebook)

Printed in United States of America

CW

10 9 8 7 6 5 4

Passport to Reading titles are leveled by independent reviewers applying the standards developed by Irene Fountas and Gay Su Pinnell in *Matching Books to Readers: Using Leveled Books in Guided Reading*, Heinemann, 1999.

ILLUMINATION PRESENTS

DESPICABLE ME 3

Best Boss Ever

Adapted by Trey King

Based on the Motion Picture Screenplay by
Cinco Paul and Ken Daurio

LITTLE, BROWN AND COMPANY
New York   Boston

Minions have walked the earth

for millions of years.

They are looking for the perfect master.

Once, the Minions called a T. rex their master.
But he fell into a volcano by mistake.
Oops!

The Minions' next master was a caveman.
They helped him hunt wild animals—
until a wild animal hunted him.

The Minions helped build the pyramids in Egypt.
But they read the plans upside down.
A pyramid fell on their new master.

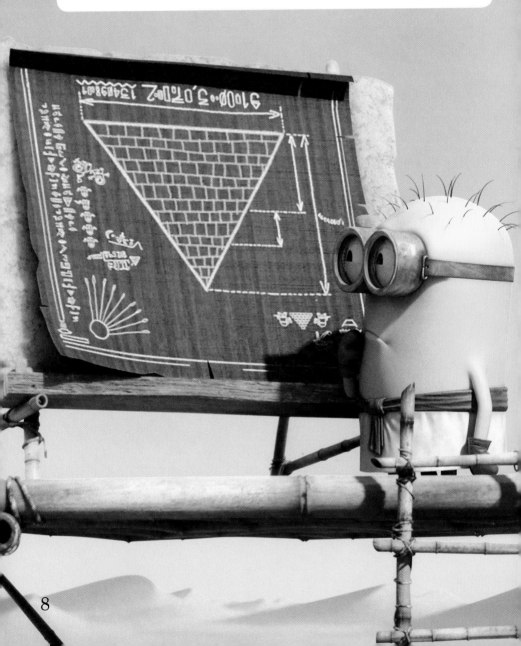

Their next boss was the famous
vampire, Dracula.

They opened the window
to let some sunlight in.
That was a bad idea.

The Minions have had lots of masters.
None of them ever stuck around for
very long.

There was always a shark or a cannon or something that got in the way.

Then they met Scarlet Overkill.
They thought they had found
their best master ever.

But she turned out to be a little too mean.

Finally, they met Gru.
They worked in the secret
lab under his house.

Gru was a despicable villain.

He had big plans to steal the moon!

It would be the biggest heist in all history!

The Minions love trouble.

They helped Gru steal a shrink ray.

(He needed it to shrink the moon.)

But another villain, Vector,
stole the shrink ray from Gru.
Gru and the Minions needed
to get it back.

That is how Gru and the Minions
met three orphaned girls named
Margo, Edith, and Agnes.

Gru and the Minions got the shrink ray
back and stole the moon.

But Gru traded it all to become a father.

The Minions helped take care of the girls.

They made breakfasts—and messes.

They tucked the girls in at night.

They also helped Gru with his business,
making jams and jellies.
The Minions made a mess there, too.

When Gru met Lucy,

he became a super spy.

He was too busy being in love

to notice someone was taking

his Minions.

El Macho changed the Minions
into purple monsters.

Gru went after the evil Minions.

He had to save them.

But how?

His homemade jelly

may have tasted gross,

but it changed the Minions

back to normal.

Now the Minions are tired
of being heroes.
They miss being villains.
Mel leads them on strike!

Well, except for Jerry and Dave.

Jerry and Dave get to play
with pigs in Freedonia.

Meanwhile, Mel and
the Minions get hungry.
After they take some pizza,
they end up in jail.

Jail is terrible.

Mel and the other Minions

miss Gru.

Gru was the best boss ever!
Once they get out of jail,
they are going to make things right.

Attention, Minions fans!
Go back and read this story again—
but this time, see if you can find these words!
Can you spot them all?

T. rex

pyramid

shrink ray

pigs